Short Not Sweet

A Mini Collection

Chia L. Strickland

Copyright © 2025 by Chia L. Strickland

All rights reserved.

This book is a work of fiction. The characters, incidents, and dialogue are drawn from the author's imagination and are not to be constructed as real. Any resemblance to actual events or person, living or dead, is entirely coincidental and not intended by the author.

No part of this short story may be used or reproduced in any manner whatsoever without written permission by the publisher except in the case of brief quotations embodied in critical articles and reviews.

This story was written by a human author and edited by humans. No AI was used to produce any part of this project, including the cover image. The author does not grant permission to use her work to train any form of AI.

Book Cover Design by Chia L. Strickland.

ISBN 978-1-967564-08-8

Author's Notes

I planned to wait until I had a bigger catalog before I released my first collection. And yet, here it is. My first mini collection, set free into the world and made up of the short stories published during my first author year. Initially I thought I was just going to slap these three stories together, get a cover done or create one myself and let it go. The main purpose, I thought, was to offer my shorts to readers in print. And not only in print but in the same space so you could experience the different sides of me (so far), all at once.

However, proof after proof, I realized something. This mini collection isn't for just the readers—it's also for me. 2025 was the year that I pushed beyond the imposter syndrome and published something tangible. I finished a project, and then another one, and then another one! They're no longer just stories sitting on a hard drive. My first year isn't done and it's been tough and rewarding so far. And I'm just getting started.

So this collection is a love letter to myself and a thank you to my readers. While putting this together, I've spent some extra time with these three stories, revamped and re-edited them a little. The originals will still be available in eBook format, but I hope that all the little adaptations I've made, make reading these short stories that much more enjoyable.

This short story follows the swift disintegration of society which begins with the corruption of one man. Hinrich Callaghan is rotten to his core and doesn't care what happens as his wickedness spreads from person to person—on the contrary, it's something he enjoys. But how he deals with the ramifications of a world where everyone is just like him, is not how he imagined he would.

The Day the World walked into The Sea

Throughout every iteration of the world, there consistently exists an infinite variety of expressions of humanity but never in history has there lived a human as nasty as Hinrich Callaghan. Dressed in the best money could buy with a watch on his wrist that costed more than his housekeeper could make in two years, Hinrich adjusted his glasses as he peered out at the metropolis below him.

He smiled a crookedly handsome smile before he walked back to his desk in the corner suite office and admired the menagerie of family photos he displayed there—his monstrosity of a daughter, the son he'd nurtured into the perfect bully and his superficial, compassionless wife. His crooked smile slowly expanded.

Hinrich wasn't the only nasty person alive but if you collected every one of the vile, from horizon to horizon and tested them like laboratory mice, Hinrich would be the worst. A man not older than forty-three he was as malicious as could be. The degeneration of his soul and any goodness he once held had wilted into a putrefying odor of despair and anger which always lingered on his skin. But never once was he deterred by it, he simply covered it up with deodorant and alluring fragrances, lathering on coconut and lavender oils after his showers.

If you looked very closely at him for a long time, a person would see his handsome face wasn't quite right. Any of his staff could tell you and they whispered among themselves about him whenever he was away. His eyes though bright looked like they had been darted into the sockets at the corners by a seamstress. His too white teeth, perfect at first glance, appeared too thin at their bases where they attached to his gums. And his bones were all too bony, a lot of them slightly protruding from beneath the thin skin of his face. But he was still handsome and he wore glasses to distract from his eyes though he could see perfectly well, and never smiled his crooked smile too widely, to hide his teeth. His spray tans were scheduled five times as often as the average tans should be since he needed to camouflage the bones pressing unnaturally against his skin.

From the desk in his office in that corner suite, he initiated orders to perpetuate large scale environmental warfare—satisfaction blooming in his chest from knowing the precise amount of toxins leaking out of his factories all over the world, into founts of natural drinking water. Tears of happiness threatening to spring free at the thought of polluting the air and how many would choke and die on it before their 20th birthdays. He rubbed his spiteful hands together watching the signature ink dry before he got up, switched his glasses for sunglasses and walked to the elevator—making his way home to the horrible little family he'd built.

In his cold, contemporary mansion, Hinrich and his collective did all the things a normal family would do. They had dinner and he asked them about their day. They had dessert, reminisced and laughed at inside family jokes. And after his children went to bed and his wife to do late-night yoga, Hinrich went to the basement.

He descended the barely lit acrylic stairs and locked the door behind him, sucking the sound below into the room when the door clicked close. Then he walked the hallway in darkness hitting the glass windows like a petulant child in the reptile habitat at a zoo. But Hinrich's cages held something more sinister than vipers and constrictors. When he got to the last window on the left, he squatted down so he was eye level with the occupant watching as she held her sweaty forehead against the cool glass.

"Why? Why are you doing this? Please let me go." But Hinrich didn't answer. He just smiled his crooked smile, then sat on the floor. He sat there until midnight, waiting for her shakes to start and listened to the noises from the others as he waited.

On Wednesday, Hinrich stayed at home as his family set out for the day. He'd told his daughter to offer the new girl a piece of gum with a small razor inside, gave his son a *special cocktail* for that "playing hard to get" girl at the party he was going to later and slapped his wife on her ass. Then told them to go out and not to come back if they didn't make him proud that day. Because Hinrich Callaghan was the worst of the worst and whenever he could spread his nastiness, he spread it to the best of his ability.

At 11AM on Wednesday, Hinrich slammed the new housekeeper against the wall next to the basement door when she'd jiggled the handle in an attempt to open the door.

"What the fuck are you doing?" The question a treacherous threat as her head hit the concrete. His bony fingers reached around to the back of her neck and he dug his fingernails into her skin.

"Lo siento mucho. ¿No se supone que debemos limpiar ahí?" Her voice quivered.

"No, you don't *limpia esta habitación*. You understand?"

Her involuntary whimper made his crooked smile grow and he ran his free hand up the side of her skirt and let it linger there as her fear started to muddle together with the pungent odor of his skin.

"Yes, yes sir. I—I, understand." He let her go.

Hinrich was pleased and his gratification relaxed him in the same instant that it ignited the vile within the housekeeper. So without meaning to and in a way that he never had before, Hinrich spread his nastiness to someone else and she was let loose into the world when she left.

Her first day on the job she couldn't offer to quit and she'd been assaulted and scared shitless by the client. She'd brought it up to the others, in an attempt to gather evidence in case anyone else shared the same encounter as she had. If she could take it to the owner of the company then maybe at best, a pattern of behaviour could be reported—at the least, she wouldn't have to go back to that house even if he was the biggest client. But the small group of her co-workers looked to the floor and through the windows, avoiding her gaze.

A couple of them shook their heads and someone said, "We don't say anything and we never go near that door." But she wasn't sure who.

As they filed out for the day someone slipped a piece of paper into her hand. And as soon as she climbed into her car, she read it.

> *The last girl who complained and reported him to the police disappeared. So either quit or be quiet about it.*

She cussed and shoving the piece of paper into her center console, started her car. She'd pulled out of the parking lot and had barely driven fifteen minutes before someone in a rush rear-ended her—she cussed again. And the nastiness that had lodged itself deep in her heart started to grow roots there, and she became a little more like Hinrich.

The vile spread and it spread more quickly than anyone, including Hinrich Callaghan could have imagined. And he didn't know it was because of him but seeing a little bit of the vile behind the eyes of more everyday people was euphoric for him.

The increase in crime was astonishing and the hatred in the world was so palpable that he would swear he could feel it along his bony fingers as he passed his hand through open air. He would walk by people in the streets and smell the decomposing stench of their goodness seeping through their skin. He started wondering when people would notice. And soon enough, he realized that everyone else was becoming aware. Videos popped up all over the internet. In the beginning the podcasts and protests were rampant, but slowly the numbers dwindled as the vile spread.

And people died. The first murder directly tied to the actions of the vile spread by Hinrich, sent a shock wave through him and jolted him awake at 3 AM on a random Thursday morning. Hinrich was electric and at some point his eisce was awoken. He accepted the spread of infectious wickedness as one of his productions, though he didn't know exactly how he'd done it.

At 4 PM on the following Saturday, his horrible little family was sitting by their pool when a group of his son's friends arrived to hang out. He and his washed-out wife got up to make their way inside when the odious smell of the vile wafted through the air. His head spun around but he couldn't figure out who it was coming from before it was too late. The "playing hard to get" girl had infiltrated the group and jabbed a knife into his son's neck, before anyone realized she was there and what her plan was. She retracted it quickly as a stream of crimson liquid pulsed from the wound. His perfectly molded rapist, bully of a son fell back into the pool—his blood dispersing across the surface before permeating the body of chlorine water, altering the section surrounding the fresh corpse.

His wife screamed and his bestial daughter pulled her leg out of the water before the blood could reach her. Chaos erupted and Hinrich continued walking inside, with a handsomely crooked smile.

No one showed up to move the body and Hinrich caught his wife dragging it out a week later with tears streaming down her face, and he was disgusted. Her weakness, revolting since they could always make more monsters if they wanted. And he knew that now, those monsters would be even more perfect because the vile was everywhere.

The population was decreasing drastically. People with the vile were murdering people without it as much as they were killing each other. And the people without the vile, who had survived attacks or had avoided being attacked, weren't living long anymore. By the sparse reporting still floating around in the world, it sounded like they just disappeared.

Then his wife—his vapid and callous wife just disappeared—he'd found a chalky essence of her existence arranged around and through her clothes that laid on their cobalt blue sectional. That was three days after their daughter came home with her eye gouged out. She had died in her room from a stab wound someone had given her. They didn't know she'd been stabbed, and by the time he went to check on her and the eye, she was dead on the bathroom floor.

Hinrich had found his daughter's body and just closed the door, then told his wife who laid on the couch wailing. He left her alone, unwilling to subject himself to her crying, and when he returned—she was a pile of chalk. He sat down, finished his old fashioned, then went to bed. Lulled to sleep by the magnitude of the growing vile he could always feel thundering in his chest.

The reports stopped soon after and then there was no communication from anywhere or by anyone. There was just Hinrich and the vile.

Never in history has there lived a human as nasty as Hinrich Callaghan except for the time Hinrich had spread his nastiness so far and wide that the only people who existed were exactly like Hinrich. And when all the people were exactly like Hinrich, all everyone knew or felt was the vile.

The vile became more concentrated within them as fewer and fewer of them remained. It grew, entwining its roots deep within their psyche until all they felt was the compulsion for more. Everyone except Hinrich, who at every given moment was being fed an unlimited stream of their violence and degeneration because he had started the infection.

Then, there were only three of them left in the world. Hinrich felt the precise moment when number three killed number two, then started to make their way to him. He didn't know who was coming but *they were coming* and it was exhilarating.

It took her approximately ten days to reach his front gate and when she pushed it open, the heavy metal creaked with the motion. She walked up the long driveway past the overgrown bushes and plants until she was standing in the entryway. She walked into the living room and found Hinrich sitting next to clothes laid out on the chair, the faint outline of chalky substance still visible. As he sipped his bourbon, he turned his head to look his final, perfect specimen in the face.

He laughed at the revelation—a twisted and hollow sounding thing. The echo creating a din of discomfort in the air when his laughter bounced off the walls.

"I should have guessed it would have been you!" His voice overwhelming jovial.

The housekeeper curled her lip up at his crooked smile and stepped around until she was standing feet away, but directly in front of where Hinrich sat.

Then she lunged for him and he lunged for her.

The fight didn't last very long or maybe it lasted longer than any documented fight. And when it was done, Hinrich sprawled next to her unmoving body. The trickle of blood from her head was still running down the side of her face, and her top was torn. He propped himself up on his right arm, which was closest to her, and used his left to look at the fingerprints around her neck.

When he got up, the nasty thing that he was, he kicked her one more time and laughed to himself at the underwear around her knees. He grabbed the bottle of bourbon that had somehow survived "the clash of the titans" and walked down the hill to the beach.

Hinrich walked the short distance admiring all the vile had done. He was the only one left, just him and the vile, in the whole world. He was the world. And as he reached the beach the realization dawned on him, that there was nothing else to feed the vile.

It pulsed under his skin and the mephitic smell, gushing out of his pores. He'd taken the vile and spread it so far, it had morphed into some starved, gargantuan thing. Then it all came home to him and it moved furiously in him seeking more but there was nothing left to give it.

The vile that made Hinrich Callaghan so proud to be so destructive, started to atrophy. And as it faded, his panic grew. Not his goodness because that was gone, had been gone for a very long time, even though he was only forty-three.

The last of the vile diminished on a Monday morning at 4:26 AM as Hinrich sat on the beach. The void it left, filled to capacity with the deplorable things he had done. He was still the nastiest person to ever exist and now he was the only person that would ever exist again. He was nasty and void of goodness but overflowing with the memories of the vile. So Hinrich got up and finished his bottle of liquor. He shattered the glass against a rock, took a shard and plunged it into his stomach.

Then Hinrich Callaghan—the last person alive in the entire world—walked into the sea.

BOUGAINVILLEA ISLE

The people of Bougainvillea Isle have a secret and every other country in the world is dying to know what it is. After practically disappearing from the world stage decades ago, the island is now ready to open its borders to only one person.

Chasity Cross is the first visitor to the island in twenty years, but will Chasity discover the secrets of the isle before her time is up?

Bougainvillea Isle

The quaint island of Bougainvillea was a tourist honeypot in the late 70's until it seemingly vanished off the face of the earth, closing its borders to all incoming traffic. Newspaper articles around the world printed the official statement from the president of the island even though no substantial information was given. *"World loses Prized Gem"* was the headline most people remember reading.

During that time reporters from everywhere attempted contact—every one champing at the bit to write the elusive story of what exactly happened in the society now cut off from the rest of the world. Each one of them unsuccessful in their attempts. This went on for a few years, until everyone gave up on the idea that anyone would find or figure out anything about the circumstances surrounding the occurrence. Bougainvillea was allowed to do what its inhabitants had set out to accomplish and the entire nation drifted into isolation.

Cruise ships and pilots would point it out as a passing attraction when they went by. Occasionally some billionaire attempted to go to the island with the idea that they would be allowed to explore it or even purchase the isle so they could find out its secrets. Their attempts were as unsuccessful as the reporters before them; most having damaged their yachts or sea planes in the venture to surreptitiously dock on the island's shores.

Bougainvillea Isle, where the water is so blue and clear you can see the shells on the bottom of the ocean floor. The environment is so warm and welcoming, the entire island feels like home. And coconut trees litter the sides of every major street. A place where the sun is constantly shining and the breezes caress you when they blow sea salt across your skin. The island everyone wants to know about.

No one had heard from an inhabitant of Bougainvillea until twenty years after their self-imposed shut out, when President Egbert Hollis made it known that he was open to negotiations with another country. The proposal: once a quarter, the isle would trade resources only found on their land mass for specific resources on a prearranged list. When the offer was first released, most people assumed it was a prank. But President Hollis sent out invitations following the initial proposal, inviting the leaders of the five neighbouring countries to meet for formal discussions. Invitees were not allowed to proceed beyond the sandy shores of the meeting point but Hollis needed to make sure that the world knew he was serious, and Bougainvillea Isle was back—at least in some small capacity for now.

The day after the meeting, "*Thaw in Freeze Out?*" was splashed across the pages of every major paper. And following the news, an impressive number of countries were open to the idea of sharing resources with the isle especially if that meant they had access to Bougainvillea's sugar, gold, and fisheries.

It took approximately three weeks to reach an agreement and when Bougainvillea set out their stipulations of trade, the world was astonished and intrigued. The island was willing to trade thirty-five percent of their fish, twenty percent of their sugar and three percent of their gold. In addition, the government of Bougainvillea would allow a citizen of their newly partnered country to visit the island for four days. The list of the items President Hollis requested were kept secret from the public—but the leader of the partnering island accepted the terms. No one outside the contract would know whether the list from Hollis contained five items or twenty, but one thing was certain—any leader presented with the opportunity would have accepted whatever Hollis asked for, at the chance to figure out firsthand what happened two decades ago.

After weeks of constant conversations, the travel arrangements were officially finalized. But some hours before the shipment exchange, Hollis announced that the visiting citizen could not be the country's head of state themselves or anyone with a political position. The person also had to show proof of being a citizen of the selected country and not an individual flown in for an auctioned off chance at seeing the isle. Chancellor Miriam Cross, whose country was selected for the partnership, was peeved—having planned to go herself. However, due to the stipulations set by the agreement with Hollis, which included his ability to change the conditions around the visitation at will, she decided to send her daughter.

Chasity Cross stepped off the delivery ferry in pink heels and slicked back ponytail with a duffle bag slung over her shoulder. Outside was warm—the humidity overwhelmingly thick and stifling, she was glad she hadn't listened to her mother's packing advice. Halfway down the pier she paused to take off the light cardigan she was wearing. Chasity tied it around her waist, took off her shoes and hoisted the duffle bag back up. She was sweating, her bag was heavy and she was having an all-around bad time so far—nobody had even shown up to get her.

She made her way off the pier and stood at the edge of the beach where the sand touched the cement of the road. Her bag strap was digging into the top of her shoulder but she didn't want to get it dirty by dropping it on the ground. She glanced down at her feet, disgusted at the white dust already accumulating on her toes. Back up the pier she could hear the crew from the ferry talking to the dock crew, both sets of people trying to solve the logistics of shifting shipping containers back and forth.

Eventually Chasity dropped the bag, took the cardigan from around her waist and used the arms to dab the sweat off her face. She then dusted the sand from her feet and tried to clean the white cast off her toes before stepping back into her heels. Her mother would be mortified if she'd heard Chasity met the president as a disheveled mess.

She'd just finished pulling out the pink, bow scrunchie from her hair when a police-escorted car rounded the corner to her left. It came to a stop directly in front of her and a gentleman got out. He took a couple steps towards her and extended his hand.

"I'm President Hollis. Welcome to the isle!"

Chasity shook his hand, introduced herself and started getting into the car after the driver had taken her bag.

"I don't make a habit of being late but my son apparently lost the ability to be ready on time." Hollis slid in after her, and only as the door closed did Chasity lay eyes on the president's incredibly attractive son.

"Chasity, this is Mateo. He'll be your escort over the next four days." Mateo winked at her then smiled as the vehicle moved off.

Chasity was leaning against the car door watching the foliage outside whisk by. It was just as her mother had described to her, despite the fact that her mother had never seen the island herself. Coconut trees framed the roads, cradled between the abundance of lush greenery and flowering plants. They passed locals walking with baskets of fruit on their heads and others setting up vendor stands by the roadside. She asked a passing question about why there was no traffic.

"Most people bike or walk, we don't have a lot of cars on the island." A haphazard nod was her only response since Mateo was making her nervous.

She continued looking through the window, painfully aware of the two brown eyes that had been staring at her the entire car ride. His gaze made her feel fidgety—she held her left index finger between her right index finger and thumb so she could discreetly stroke her matte, pink nail polish. Her eyes focused squarely on the passing scenery outside with the kaleidoscope of butterflies in her stomach fluttering around at accelerated speed.

"Stop staring." President Hollis kept telling his son who would chuckle and look away for a nanosecond before she could feel his gaze on her again.

The drive from the pier was relatively brief. It took them around twenty minutes to make it to their destination. Hollis was constantly pointing out "must see" locations or spewing random facts about the island, clearly enthralled by the opportunity to act as a professional tour guide.

"No worries, Mateo will show you everything you need to see!" He would say excitedly, before taking a minuscule break which served as a launch pad into a new historically focused monologue.

During the entire time, Mateo kept looking at Chasity and Chasity kept looking through the car window.

When the driver made a rash left turn, Chasity closed her eyes, steeled herself and braced for impact until she realized the turn hadn't been into the giant tree she'd been admiring.

"The tree provides an optical illusion to the road that leads up to the entrance of the house," he wasn't laughing but she could hear the smile in his voice.

"Oh." A simple response to avoid more embarrassment, as the heat of mortification warmed her neck.

They drove the next five minutes in silence—through the security gate and up the extra long driveway, into an expansive courtyard that sat nicely in front of a mansion.

"Welcome to our home." President Hollis said proudly.

Chasity got out of the car and gaped at the colossal presidential compound as she examined her surroundings.

Mateo had barely gotten to the first step of the stone staircase when a slender woman with deep terracotta skin busted through the iron, double entry doors. Mrs. Hollis had warm, dark brown, almond-shaped eyes that twinkled slightly whenever she smiled at Chasity, which happened quite a lot in the short space of time since they'd met. She kept asking Chasity if she had a comfortable trip even though Chasity kept confirming her trip was fine. They walked up the stairs and into an airy foyer accented with a mahogany table that held a large crystal vase. The vase was adorned with Baby Blue Eucalyptus, Lavender, Pampas grass and dried blue Bougainvillea flowers.

When her bag was brought in, Chasity was led to her room and left alone to settle in. The room matched the overall aesthetic of the Hollis's presidential residence. A king-sized bed sat between two large, floor length windows with tan window jambs. The bed, framed by a spindled cedar headboard, was made up with white sheets which were partially covered by an immense dusty rose blanket. The bed itself was positioned between two large windows. It was flanked by side tables carved out of the same wood as the bedframe. The table on the left held a smaller arrangement of the grand display in the foyer, while the one on the right held a simple spherical lamp housed in a gold base. The gold base on the table matched the frame of a large hoop mirror hanging on the wall over the headboard. On her way to a plush loveseat that matched the blanket in colour, she passed a large walk-in closet with cedar wooden doors. But what caught her eye most was the impressive ensuite bathroom she couldn't wait to enjoy. Outside there was a balcony with a wrap-around wrought iron balcony that looked out towards the ocean. Chasity squealed delightfully, then ran to take a shower.

After unpacking and a nap, the housekeeper knocked on her door summoning her to dinner. The entire Hollis family sat at an elaborate dining table having multiple small conversations. Mateo was laughing with a girl she hadn't met before, who looked a lot like him. Mrs. Hollis was tending to a toddler Hollis, and Mr. Hollis—he'd asked to be called Mr. instead of president—was waving her further into the dining room.

"Chasity, this is my sister Maya—"

"His older sister!" Maya cut Mateo off.

"By two minutes." The twin said in unison but with vastly different emotional intonations.

"And this wild one is Madelyn." Mrs. Hollis cut in from across the table as she tilted her head towards the little girl who was trying to push a carrot into her ear.

"So, are you coming to the bonfire?" Maya asked just as Chasity was taking a bite of the food which had not too long been delivered to them.

"Bonfire?" She asked after she'd swallowed the chicken.

"A whole car ride and you didn't invite her to the bonfire?" Maya threw a napkin at her brother. "I have to do everything around here."

"Well, I needed to see if I liked her first. Or did you want me to invite a weirdo and ruin our night?"

Dinner was uneventful, filled with mostly bickering from the twins and a compelling speech from Maya as to why Chasity was *absolutely* coming to the bonfire with them.

They ate until Chasity was stuffed. The food had been delectable, so she was disappointed when she could not finish dessert; bread pudding with a Bougainvillea rum sauce. She took a few bites and had the leftovers put aside, then went to find an outfit.

At 10 PM, Maya came into her room to inspect her outfit: blue, distressed denim shorts and a pink, crotchet crop top that was more bralette than shirt. Chasity had styled the ensemble with a gold, layered pendant necklace and a white summer appropriate cardigan. She held a pair of pink Gucci slides in her hands.

"Very cute! Now let's go, Mateo's waiting for us to walk down." Chasity snatched up her phone, even though she wouldn't have service once they were outside then followed Maya.

"Walk? This late?" Maya chuckled before answering.

"The bonfire is technically on our compound so yeah, we'll cut through some trees then double back to the shoreline. It's not too far, even though the grounds are disgustingly massive."

They met Mateo at a door that led to an immaculately designed patio. Walked past the pool, and after five minutes of landscaped grass, turned right and headed into the previously mentioned trees. Maya was up ahead and Mateo had slowed to match Chasity's pace.

"You look amazing." She almost tripped at the compliment. "I really like the navel ring." There was the smile in his voice again.

"Thanks, I got it wh—"

"We're here!" Maya announced from up ahead, obviously for Chasity's benefit.

The three of them broke through the line of trees onto a beach where they were greeted by a blazing bonfire and around twenty people.

Cheering erupted when the crowd got sight of Maya and Mateo who were promptly given beers. The two took turns introducing Chasity before Maya disappeared with her best friend. Mateo and Chasity sat together on a washed-up piece of driftwood; a piece in a circle of driftwood stationed around the bonfire.

"So *you're* the outsider?" A muscled boy wearing short shorts sat next to Mateo and leaned over. "You didn't say she was a sweet girl." He winked at Mateo who just rolled his eyes.

"I'm Ambrose." He extended his hand out towards her.

"Chasity." She shook his hand.

The two boys talked for a while until Ambrose got up to make rounds with this "party favours", leaving Chasity and Mateo sitting alone.

"How are you liking the island so far?" Mateo asked as he handed her the island's version of a space cake before popping one into his mouth. Chasity inspected it closely.

"Is it blue?"

"Yeah, from the Bougainvillea extract. Try it." She hesitated briefly then popped it into her mouth.

"You all sure love Bougainvillea here. I've never seen blue ones before." She titled her head up to look at the moon.

"Yeah, they're super rare usually. But they grow here all over the place for some reason." There was reverb on his voice. "You didn't answer my question."

"Oh, the island. I like it. Different to what I would have thought, y'know, since you folks are all cut off from the world."

Mateo took a sip of his beer and laughed. "No, no, I get it. You're the first person who wasn't born here that I've met, so *I get it.*"

Chasity hadn't even thought about the fact that she was as much of a novelty to them as they were to her.

"You all seem so normal though, why—" She started to giggle and Mateo offered her some of his beer. "Why did the island cut itself off from the rest of the world?"

"Beats me. I wasn't born yet and most people who were alive then don't talk about it. Seems like it worked out pretty fine to me." More reverb, so much reverb. She handed the bottle back.

The feeling of eyes staring at her returned; Chasity was still looking at the moon.

"You stare a lot. Did you know that?"

"Only when I see something I want." She could feel the heat run up her neck as the night breeze erected goosebumps along her legs.

She stopped looking at the moon.

"What do you want?" Her voice barely made it passed her lips.

"To do this." Mateo leaned over and kissed her.

Chasity's head swam as he deepened the kiss. Flavours of coconut and pineapple filling her senses. She pulled away, both of them dazed and smiling at each other.

"Want to go for a walk?" She nodded in response.

So ensorcelled with the idea of leaving with Mateo, Chasity missed the entertainment around the bonfire. There, a girl named Layla sat singing with a guitar:

The magic of the blue Bougainvillea So potent to you and me
Is the beauty of the isle, so hidden you can't see
It's why we taste of wonder
And wonders never cease
It's why I could just eat you up
And why you'd take a bite out of me

Layla continued singing the song and others joined in. All of them, singing and drinking, high on Ambrose's "space cakes."

And somewhere down the beach, Chasity was kissing Mateo.

It was 2 AM when the three of them reached the house and 3 AM after Mateo left her room. Chasity climbed into bed and thought of her family for the first time since she'd gotten to the island. She started drifting off to sleep thinking about how her little brother would love the island and about how she wanted her parents to move here so she could stay with Mateo. Piña colada tasting Mateo with his soft lips and softer hands. She fell into a deep sleep of the most palatable dreams.

She woke up at half past nine and noticed a note on the floor which had been slid under the door—the family was out for the morning. She was therefore welcome to grab breakfast and relax or explore until they came back, which would be around noon. The morning to herself didn't sound too bad, so after taking a shower she headed down to the kitchen where the staff made her pancakes.

When breakfast was over, Chasity set out to explore the compound. She walked almost an identical path to the bonfire. But where they had doubled back to head down to the beach, she went the opposite direction and headed into the forested area. Ten minutes into her walk, she found a small alcove which opened out into a larger cave. There was a natural saltwater pool inside. She walked further into the cave when a faint, blue glow caught her attention. Behind the pool and lining the back of the walls were hundreds of glowing blue Bougainvilleas. She reached down to pick one and had to wiggle it free from a rock. A forceful yank later, and all she'd gotten was a face full of blue pollen and a flower that had lost its glow. Sneezing, she left the cave and started making her way back to the house. It was 12:30 PM when she got back.

Maya was at the pool with a few of her friends when Chasity shuffled by. She waved as she went into the house, heading straight to her room so she could wash off the plant matter.

Mateo was waiting for her.

"You look—, you found the cave huh?" He tried to suppress his laugh.

"Sure did. Why didn't anyone tell me that you get flower bombed if you pick the flowers?"

"Cause it's only if you pick the glowy ones. And I don't know. We didn't think you would walk that far?" He was laughing now.

"Well I did, so now I have—" She stopped to sneeze again. "I have to go shower." She walked into the ensuite.

"Want company?"

She closed the door and locked it as Mateo kept laughing from outside.

Dinner that night was another fabulous assortment of food, accompanied by more twin bickering and an apology from Mr. and Mrs. Hollis regarding the family outing earlier that day. Between dinner and dessert, Mr. Hollis slid Chasity and Mateo itineraries for "Day Three". Mateo was to take her to some historical sights and show her the Bougainvillea fields.

"She found the cave today." Mateo said, smiling at his father.

"Oh." Mr. Hollis replied.

"Yup, walked right by us covered in blue dust this afternoon." Maya chimed in without looking up from her phone.

"How interesting." Mrs. Hollis replied as she fiddled with Madelyn.

The discussion felt awkward and Chasity was embarrassed. "I'm sorry if I wasn't supposed to go that far, or to pick the flowers. I was just curious—" Mr. Hollis cut her off.

"It's no bother. It's just—" He hesitated, struggling with the explanation so his wife continued.

"The flowers, the ones that glow can make people extremely sick. It's why we don't let our little ones near them. You didn't do anything wrong, I guess my husband and I were just relieved you didn't get sick." She offered Chasity a small smile.

"Oh." Was the only response Chasity could muster.

"Yes, that's it. I wouldn't want anything to happen to you while I have you on loan from your mother, dear!" He began laughing as dessert came out. "Looky here, it's my favourite! Cheesecake!"

Chasity noticed that everyone's dessert contained the telltale signs of the blue Bougainvillea extract. Everyone's except Madelyn's. Chasity ate her slice slowly as Mr. Hollis went over the itinerary some more.

"It's going to be a long day tomorrow, so make sure you both get a good night's sleep," Mr. Hollis was saying as he and his wife picked up the toddler and excused themselves from the table.

"Are you coming tomorrow?" Chasity asked Maya when the adults were gone.

"Of course not. Those tours bored me near to death when we had to do them at school. No offense, but I don't think I like anyone enough to do *that* to myself willingly." She laughed as she got up from the table, her passion braids swinging behind her as she headed out of the room. "My brother on the other hand." She winked at Chasity and left.

"I guess we should turn in too." Mateo was already getting up from the table as he spoke.

They walked up the stairs and he followed her into her room.

Mateo snuck out of her room in the early hours of the morning after they spent the entire night talking and making out. Maya caught them kissing by the bedroom door as she was coming back from an early morning swim.

"Naughty, naughty." Was all Maya said as she chuckled and disappeared into her room.

When her alarm went off, she hadn't gotten enough rest. The temptation of "just another five minutes" beckoned her back to sleep. To avoid falling into its trap, she decided to try calling her mother.

"Finally! I haven't heard you for days!" Her mother's voice was vibrant with the telltale signs that she'd had too much coffee.

"Hello to you too, mother."

"Hi Chas, morning! It is morning there, right?! What's it like? How are you?!"

"Mom, slow down. First, I texted you every day by the way. You're just too busy to respond. Yes, it's morning. It's amazing and I'm good."

Her phone started beeping—a request from her mother to switch the audio to a video call.

"You can't see me, it's still dark."

"Switch it anyway." And Chasity did. Then ended up turning on the bedside lamp to compensate for the fact that her mother was unsatisfied she couldn't *actually* see Chasity.

Chasity showed her the room and told her about the Hollis family.

"A boy? How old is this boy?"

"Don't make it weird, mother." She rolled her eyes, forgetting for a second that they were on a video call.

"Chasity Loraine!"

"Just turned nineteen."

"Chasity! You are *sixteen* years old!"

"And I'll be *seventeen* in three weeks. He's barely two years older than me. Relax —"

"Don't you tell me to relax—" A voice in the background cut her mother off.

"Excuse me, ma'am? Canada is on the phone."

"Sorry Chas—"

"Yeah I know, you've got to go. Check your messages more."

"Love you!"

"Love you too, mom." She watched her phone screen go back to its default.

Chasity didn't get a chance to tell her mother about the rare blue, glowing Bougainvillea. Something she only remembered as she was stepping into the shower to get ready for her day.

Mateo and Maya met Chasity for breakfast—their parents had already left for work and Madelyn was somewhere with the nanny. After breakfast was over Maya split, letting them know she would meet up with them later when the humdrum of the day was done.

The island seemed more humid today as Chasity tried to stop her shirt from sticking to her. She was standing on the outdoor staircase waiting for the driver. When the driver pulled a new car around, disembarked and handed the keys to Mateo, she pretended not to notice.

"Enjoy your morning off, Raph!" Mateo climbed into the driver's seat and Chasity slid into the passenger side of the SUV.

"You guys have more than one car? *How* do you have more than one car? This is a new car!" She buckled the seatbelt and said a quick prayer, making the sign of the cross in the air.

"Your faith in my driving skills is duly noted." Mateo laughed, started the engine and drove off. He never answered her questions about the cars.

President Hollis had scheduled a number of tours for them, including one that took them underground and another that explored the process for making Bougainvillea extract. Then they visited the fields where she learned that the plant in its more potent form—the glowing flowers—or in its edible forms, like the extract, was severely poisonous to children under the age of six and some adults. However, in people who could consume it, edible forms of the plant modified the taste buds temporarily which enhanced the flavour of different foods. And the more Chasity learned, the more she couldn't understand why Maya would label the tours as boring.

"That was all pretty interesting." She said, clicking the seatbelt into place. Mateo closed her door before running around to his side of the car.

"Glad you think so. Maya would have expired thirty minutes in. Ready for lunch?"

"Definitely."

While they sat and ate at the seaside bistro Mateo had told her was his favourite place to eat on the island—he made plans with Maya for later.

"She wants to do a pajama, movie night something, she said." Mateo was relaying the conversation to Chasity. "Only couples though because she doesn't 'want it to be weird.'" He shook his head as he read.

"Are we—?" She stopped herself from asking the question, which caused Mateo to look up from his phone.

"Are we, what?" He smirked. "Are we a couple?" He was too coy for his own good.

Chasity could feel the heat in her ears when he started chuckling.

"Well I've known you for three days, so I would say no. But maybe we could be." He reached for her hand.

"I wasn't asking if we were a couple. I was asking if we were going together since we're *not* a couple."

"Of course you were." He laughed again and she laughed too, slapping his hand away from hers.

When they pulled up to the courtyard, Raph the driver was standing by the fountain waiting to take back the keys.

"Good luck." He said as he got into the car and drove away.

Chasity looked at Mateo, confused, while Mateo sighed and headed up the steps. It was only after they got inside that Raph's words made sense. The entire foyer was chaos as far as her eyes could see. People were running around with decor, there was a small team making party bags, and someone walked by her wheeling a massive popcorn machine.

"I hate that your sister decides to do things so last minute." Mr. Hollis was grumbling as they walked into the kitchen.

"We're having sushi tonight for dinner before this whole thing," he waved his hand wildly through the air, "begins. Then your mother, Madelyn and I are spending the night on the east side of the property. You and Maya need to keep your friends contained."

Chasity and Mateo left his father complaining and went into the backyard where Maya had set up a silver screen and a circle of speakers that created a cordoned off area of seating. There were eight upholstered bean bag love seats and on each love seat was a little name card.

"Isn't it the cutest?!" Maya had snuck up on them and startled them both.

"It's something." Mateo looked around at all the moving parts. "Maya, *what on earth?*"

"Okay, so it wasn't supposed to be this big but then I decided why not? The set up is soon done anyway! I have popcorn machines, candy tables, nacho bars and some fully stocked coolers all over the place. Ambrose plans to bring some of his stuff and, oh crap, it's getting late—"

Maya rushed off to finish her set up while Mateo went to his room to play video games until it was time for dinner and Chasity went to relax in her room. She walked in and neatly folded on her bed was a red, lace-lined, silk nightgown and a matching robe—her name was embroidered at the edge of the belt. Instead of chilling like she'd planned, she got into bed for a nap and as sleep claimed her, she wondered how the Hollis family got all the things they had if they hadn't been trading with anyone before now.

An ornate sushi boat greeted her as she wafted into the dining room. The Hollis clan was quiet tonight and Madelyn was nowhere to be seen. Chasity wrapped her arms around herself subconsciously as she sat down—she wasn't sure what to do with the unexpected shift in the environment. No one, including Mateo, seemed to notice her at first. Instead they sat in silence, simply staring at the sushi boat. She could have sworn she saw Maya drool a little before she interrupted the peculiar behaviour.

"Impressive boat," she said with a laugh, and all at once the Hollis clan snapped out of their trance and started having conversations again.

"Remember to keep your friends contained even though I'll have two officers posted out there with you."

"That won't make it awkward at all." Maya responded to her father.

"I don't care about your cousin and his *edible depravities*, Maya —"

"Wait, Ambrose is *your cousin*?" Chasity whispered to Mateo as his sister and father kept talking.

"Yeah but it's usual— "

"Time to eat!" Mrs. Hollis ended both conversations by announcing the arrival of the food.

There was so much to eat that Chasity didn't know where to start. She reached for some yellowtail nigiri, a couple of spicy tuna pieces and a few of the native

Bougainvillea Isle sashimi. It only took five of them half an hour to eat the entire spread. When dinner was finished, the Hollis parents retired to bed, leaving the three of them to get ready for movie night.

Chasity studied her reflection in the mirror, as she stood dressed in Maya's gifted ensemble. She pulled a few of her curls apart and scrunched the sections of hair between her fingers. Then she grabbed her phone so she could message her mother. She pressed send the same time Mateo opened the door and let out a whistle. He walked over to her and kissed her, squeezing her butt through the thin silk material.

He tasted like pineapple, coconut cake and it made her a little dizzy. She started to smile while kissing him then bit his lip.

"You taste good." He pulled away and smiled back at her. "Let's go to the party."

Hours later, the movie night had morphed into a sleepover and was in full swing when Chasity and Mateo decided to go inside. The group was now starting the third movie and Ambrose had just passed out his newest version of the "space cakes", which hit them both before they made it up the stairs.

Mateo pushed her into her room and she grabbed his neck before he could even make sure the door was closed properly. Chasity pulled him to the bed and kissed him manically. His laugh sounded like ten Mateos laughing all at once and laughing forever. The reverb, amplified to a thousand.

"*You* taste like pineapple, coconut cake." She giggled to him when he was laying on top of her.

"And *you* taste like a lavender, pistachio shortbread cookie." He kissed her again.

Chasity gasped, then giggled as the world around her spun even though her eyes were closed. Her body felt good but heavy—the effects of the space cakes weighing her down into the mattress even as Mateo rolled off her.

"You taste better than Maya *for sure*. She's hot. Like ghost pepper hot honey." He turned Chasity's face to him and softly kissed her lips, then her collarbone.

"But wait, Maya? Maya's your *sister*." She put her leg over his side and he slid his hand down her back.

"*Of course* she's my *sister*. I licked her arm *once* on a dare from Ambrose. *It was awful.* Not like Mr. Parnell tonight and not like *you* now." Chasity was confused and distracted and high. He kissed her again.

"Mr. Parnell?" Her voice went up at the end of the name.

"The sushi boat—" Mateo's voice trailed off as he kissed her shoulder.

"*The sushi boat?*"

"Yeah. *That* was Mr. Parnell. Not all of it of course. But *some* of it was. Wasn't he *delicious?*"

"Oh right, uh huh. Delicious."

"Just like you."

"Just like me." Chasity kissed Mateo and bit him until his lip bled. Then she kissed him again.

Chasity was starving when she woke up alone in her room the next morning. She remembered the outstanding dinner and the movie night. She remembered almost having sex with Mateo but then not having sex with Mateo and she remembered Ambrose's space cakes. She remembered that Mateo had told her they ate someone named Mr. Parnell in the sushi boat and that he said she tasted like a pistachio lavender cookie. She recalled it all in perfect nonsensical clarity, then decided that she was most definitely *never* eating another space cake from Ambrose again.

She started gathering her things together and packing her bags—the heartache of leaving was making her movements slower than she needed them to be. The ship to take her back home was going to be at the dock in three hours and Chasity was not ready to go home. When her bag was halfway full, she went downstairs for breakfast—the whole Hollis clan was already at the table, having cheerful morning discussions. She sat down teary-eyed as the breakfast was brought out for them.

The farewell spread did not disappoint: eggs, bacon, fruit salad, and waffles topped with a mixed berry medley and Bougainvillea syrup.

"So did you have a good four days?" Mr. Hollis asked when the staff had delivered all their food.

"It was the best four days of my life." Chasity started to cry. "I miss my family so much but you've all become like a family to me and I don't want to leave."

Mrs. Hollis got up from her seat and hugged Chasity where she sat. "Well it's good that Egbert decided that you can stay. If you want. Your family can move too. Once you bring them back to visit of course *and* if they like it here."

An uncontrollable laugh pushed its way through Chasity's tears as joy filled her chest at the offer.

"You were a pleasure to have Chasity." Mr. Hollis continued. "And it's impossible to miss how smitten with you our son is." He glanced at Mateo who had been quietly sitting next to her, deflated at the thought of her leaving.

"I really hope you choose to come back." He said softly as he squeezed her hand under the table.

"She better!" Maya chimed in.

They all finished breakfast and Mateo spent the rest of the morning in her room, helping her pack and giving her kisses. When she was done packing, they met the rest of family in the foyer and Chasity said goodbye to Madelyn, Maya and Mrs. Hollis, who gave her a freshly made bento sushi box for her trip. Chasity left for the pier with Mateo and Mr. Hollis.

At 11 AM Chasity Cross boarded a ferry departing Bougainvillea Isle, and headed back to her country and her family, as the first person to visit the island since its borders closed decades before her birth. And at 11:30 AM on the same day, President Egbert Hollis addressed the citizens of his country.

"My beloved citizens, it is with pride that I announce the completion of phase one of our first human trials. 'The outsider', as she's been dubbed by the media, has successfully converted. Moreover, and by sheer happenstance, even though she was accidentally made aware of some of the details, she assumes the conversion was fictitious. The first-person account from the members of my family, including myself, can confirm that the process took three to four days when exposed to consistent amounts of the human-flower hybrid extract in food — paired with one occurrence of overwhelming exposure directly from the source plant.

When my predecessor closed the borders, the decision was made to protect the world so we could understand our new way of life. When the glowing blue flowers spontaneously appeared overnight that fateful day decades ago, they tried to eradicate them—stating that the effects were doing more harm than good. Do you still have the paper clippings?! I still have them and I plan to keep them to always remind myself of the unwillingness they had to put our people first. Because today, we embrace the gift of modification and our scientists and doctors have worked on a way for us to share it!

Citizens of the Isle, I have invited the test subject back in hopes that she brings her family so we may begin phase two of testing. Patient zero not only began to experience full modification of her taste receptors. She also displayed consistent appetite growth, and we believe this to be true—developed her own specialty flavour due to direct exposure to the source plant at full bloom. My son was able to confirm that her flavour was a combination expression—which we know is only currently represented in eighteen percent of the island's population—instead of the more common singular expression. If conversion of the entire Cross family is successful, we will welcome them into our population and expand trade negotiations. Unfortunately, my son has established a meaningful relationship with Chasity and has requested we keep her and her family from the draw if they decide to join us. And of course, until the entire transition is complete, the draw will have to regrettably continue. But I hope that in the near future, our citizens will no longer have to make 'the sacrifice' because we will have converts to replace us.

Now let's turn our attention to the Parnell family to thank them for their donation. He was absolutely divine."

The vice president stepped forward with a randomizer, hit "select" and waited for the system to choose the next citizen of Bougainvillea Isle. The names circulated on a giant screen for the individuals who attended the announcement in person, and across the TV screens of everyone who was watching from their homes. Soon the name "Scarlett Dawe" illuminated all the screens in bright green letters.

"Thank you for your sacrifice Scarlett. Please report to the medical clinic for assignment date and flavour profile testing. Soon we shall move forward to a brighter day!"

The broadcast ended.

On a ship in the ocean, Chasity was video calling her mother to tell her about their official invitation to visit the island as a family—she was expressing how bittersweet it felt to be on her way home as she ate her Mr. Parnell bento box with a blue Bougainvillea flower tucked behind her ear.

WHOLE LOTTA HEART

In Barbadian folklore, there exists an entity people call the heartman. Some think he's pure fact and some speculate he's nothing but fiction. Those who believe, say he's a malevolent spirit who roams the earth looking for victims. While others give caution that he's closer than you think.

Jamar Pilgrim is a 23-year-old man fixated on the idea that his life will improve once he has the money required to fix all his financial problems. He has become consumed by jealousy at the success his agemates are experiencing. As his luck might have it, he receives an unexpected opportunity he simply can't refuse.

Now he must reap the hearts of the innocent if he wants to get out of poverty before he ends up dead, or worse!

The Lore of The Heartman

In Barbadian folklore, there exists an entity people call the heartman. Some think he's pure fact and some speculate he's nothing but fiction. Those who believe, say he's a malevolent spirit who roams the earth looking for victims. While others give caution that he's closer than you think; he could be your brother, your nephew, a son, a best friend. A man who makes a deal with the devil and becomes something darker than what he once was. Who has no problem reaping the hearts of everyone around him, so he can acquire what he's been promised. You might believe he's real, or you might not, but the lore warns you of travelling lonely roads at night. It promises children who misbehave, especially those who wander far from home, that they may lead the heartman straight to their door.

Part One

Chapter One

The Pedestrian Experience

"Last stop." The raspy voice of the bus driver snapped me out of my daydreaming as the massive machine started slowly rolling to a halt.

I didn't plan on moving until I heard the "psst" sound of the compression brakes, and felt the slight jerk of the vehicle finally stopping. There was no rush for me to get out of the air conditioning before I had to, since I would be trading comfort to walk the rest of the way home in the blistering sun.

The bus doors opened and I stepped out—the heat from the concrete rising up to punch me in the mouth.

"Yea', thanks Roddy." The older man grumbled his salutations in response before closing the doors behind me.

Roddy started driving away; the bus pushing hot, gray exhaust towards my face. I coughed and moved to stand under a nearby tree so I could watch Roddy maneuver the bus in his attempt to turn it around. Roddy was old, stocky, and grumpy most days, but he was an amazing driver. He reoriented the machine perfectly on the first try. Five minutes later he was tapping the horn as he flew past me in the opposite direction towards town.

I took a deep breath and stepped out from under the shade of the tree into the scorching afternoon sun.

The breeze was scarce, which only made outside feel hotter than it was. The heat was stifling, and warped my usual twenty-minute jaunt into a journey that felt three decades long. I kept my eyes on the ground as I trudged up the road, constantly wiping the sweat from my brow with an old, black-and-white bandana.

Joy filled my heart when my front door came into view as I rounded the familiar corner that led to my house. And about four minutes later I was turning the knob and stepping into the solace of my living room. My shirt was drenched. I wanted to peel it off as soon as I'd locked the door behind me, but I didn't want to risk dripping sweat across my mother's floor. So, I dropped my bag on the table, took off my shoes and walked straight into the bathroom to shower off the "pedestrian experience".

Chapter Two

Always Flights. Never Feelings.

The afternoon blew by more quickly than I had noticed and before I knew it, it was four o'clock. I could tell from the noise my family was making as they came barreling into the house.

"Jay, you home?"

"Yes mummy, he home. Look he nasty bag on de table!" I could hear my mother and younger brother conversing, even though my bedroom was located at the back of the house.

Our house wasn't big. My younger brother shared a bedroom with me, and my little sister slept in the same room as our mother. We had a small kitchen, an even smaller living room and we all shared one bathroom.

Often I would go out into the yard to bathe with a hose if someone else was in the shower.

"I in de bedroom mum." I finally yelled back at the sound of her heavy footsteps already coming my way.

She opened the door and popped her head inside. "You pay de bills today, right?"

My mother looked prettier when she wasn't so tired. But years of being the sole provider had worn her down; rewarding her with dark, unrelenting bags under her eyes, and deep wrinkles before her time. When I *really* looked at her, the knot in my stomach made me wish I could do more to help. I was old enough to shoulder some of her burden. But I was the "man of the house", still in the position of a boy.

"Yea' mum, all dem pay."

"Oh good, cause ya know de bank holiday tomorra and I ain' waan nobody cutting off nuttin' in hay." She chuckled as her head disappeared into the cramped hallway.

I stared at the semi-closed door, then went back to doom scrolling on my phone while my siblings fought and screamed bloody murder.

"Mummy, tell she behave!"

"I gine tell mummy on you instead!" The sound of tiny feet slapping against the wooden floors was dispersed between the shouting. "Mummy!"

My mother didn't answer either of their pleas, and they kept fighting until eventually she clicked on the television and silenced them both.

Guess who bought a house today?!
New car, who dis?
Always flights, never feelings.

I double-tapped every captioned photo as jealousy lit a flame hotter than the sun in my chest. I couldn't even get a job, but all the people my age appeared to be living high on the hog. My mother was struggling, our house was falling apart and I was a twenty-three-year-old sharing a bedroom with my thirteen-year-old brother. I didn't know how much longer I could do this because poverty was all I'd ever known, and I was tired of being poor.

Chapter Three

Who's The Heartman?

"Tonight, I gine call de heart man fuh you!"

My brother and little sister were still going at it. I used my phone to check the time, rolled out of bed and pulled out my outfit, tossing it over the back of the chair which sat in the corner of my room.

I could hear my mother rustling around in the kitchen as she prepared dinner. She was gossiping on the phone to the soundtrack of clanking pots and pans.

"No girl, I tell ya I see she husband wid dat young girl. Ms. Graham granddaughter." A cacophony of utensils clattered between the exposé. "Mmhmm, de one dat not too long left school."

I returned to bed, prompted by tiredness that had descended out of nowhere, when the sound of little footsteps running down the hall let me know I wouldn't be taking a nap. The bedroom door flew open aggressively on her arrival.

"Mar-mar, who's de heartman?" She never waited for invitations and didn't understand the concept of knocking.

My little sister asked the question as she was climbing into my bed; I delayed answering to maintain my pretend sleep. I'd closed my eyes when I'd heard her coming. She plopped down harshly on my stomach, then used her little fingers to manually open one of my eyelids.

"Mar-mar, you sleeping? Wake up!"

"Girl, take your nasty sucker-fingers out my eye." I laughed and softly pushed her hand away, which sent those germy fingers straight back into her mouth.

"Who is de heartman?" She asked the question again. This time around, the fingers in her mouth distorted and muffled the words.

"Who tell you 'bout de heartman?" I was feigning ignorance, not interest. I liked spending time with my little sister, especially because little children were customarily ignored by adults when they tried having conversations. It always made me feel bad for them. So I made it my responsibility to indulge her discussions and now I was giving her the opportunity to tell me the story and express her feelings. Even if I already knew exactly what she was talking about.

"Akeel. He tell me he gine call de heartman fuh me." I didn't know how to respond, knowing she would only ask again. And I believed that lying to the people you loved when they needed information only made them look like idiots.

"Well," I started and paused, not sure how to phrase this for a child her age. It took a minute for me to continue and I could feel her impatience growing as she shifted around.

"De heart man is a man who does come to punish children who don't listen—"

"But I ain' hard ears!" Her small voice cut off my explanation so she could preemptively declare her innocence.

"I know, but ya ask so I telling ya. You don' waan know?" She nodded and laughed, giving me the go ahead to continue.

"Well, de heartman does come for bad-behaved children and tek way dem hearts." A tiny gasp escaped her. "But don' worry. Dat's only if ya bad-behaved like Akeel."

"You sure, right?" She bounced off my stomach and threw herself onto the pillow next to me.

"I don' look sure?" Reaching over, I tickled her until any idea of a heartman pursuing her was washed away by her happy shrieking.

When she was panting between giggles and unable to completely catch her breath, I released her so she could go play.

Chapter Four

UPSIDES TO LIVING ON AN ISLAND

It was a little after five o'clock when my brother burst through the door with the mustiness he brought from school and a grand declaration.

"Mummy say you gotta carry me wid you today!" A satisfactory smile brimming on his acne filled face.

I scoffed at him. "Mummy could say whatever she waan say. You ain' coming nowhere behind me, boss." I was drying my skin after my second shower.

My brother dropped his school bag and rushed out of the door yelling for our mother to have her rectify the situation. I pulled my dark green T-shirt over my head while I listened to his complaints in the distance.

When I was ready, I entered the living room and headed towards the door to put on my shoes.

"Jamar, car' him wid ya nuh." Her request was a plea rather than a demand.

"Nah mummy. I liming wid de men. Wuh I doing bringing a lil boy wid me? And you know he tell Kimberly de heartman gine come fuh she?" I opened the door and stood in the doorframe as I waited for her response. The sun was setting and taking most of the heat with it, ushering in a slightly chilly breeze.

"Oirt, ga long." I quickly closed the door, catching the beginning of my mother yelling at my brother about filling my sister's head with folly and tripe.

The walk to the beach was short, one of the upsides to living on an island. I was shuffling through a track that would fade into a stretch of sand. I'd barely gotten onto the beach but I could already hear the chatter of my friends.

"Pilly, that's you?!"

"Sus crioss shotta!" My friend Ross exclaimed. "Man fit hard hard ya!"

I was wearing a T-shirt, faded board shorts and some old slides. It was nothing special but Ross was the friend who exaggerated everything and hyped everyone up all the time.

"Yea' men. Gine on?" I sat down on the edge of an exposed brick after knocking some other people I knew.

"So wunna got to get in on dis fuh real." A voice I hadn't heard before was talking and everyone was focused on the sermon.

It took a little while before I was able to locate the person behind the voice. But when I saw him, I understood why everyone was enthralled by him. He was outfitted head to toe in designer clothes. His shirt was embroidered with a large logo from a luxury brand. The belt he was wearing had gold plates on both ends and a stacked gold chain on top, and his shoes were completely covered in small brand logos. A giant pair of solitaire diamond earrings were hanging from his ears and I didn't know much about watches, but the one on his wrist looked like it cost a small fortune.

"Wunna don't know about dis hay. But it sweet." He laughed as he shook his wrist to move the watch. I watched the diamonds dance as the watch clinked around.

This man was a stranger to me but the resentment burned in my stomach and the envy burrowed deep into my spirit. No one would ever hear me admit it, but I would do anything to be like him.

Chapter Five

Running With The Big Boys

The night progressed like a wounded sloth and I was having a shitey time. When show-and-tell was almost done, the new man announced himself to those of us who had no idea who he was. It was probably for my benefit more than anything else, since I could feel the bitterness contorting my face every time he said something. But when he finally got off of his soap box, the normal conversations resumed—filling the previously occupied space with gaffs and laughter.

At some point during the night, someone lit a spliff and we ended up in a not so symmetrical circle with mister decked-out-in-designer sitting closest to me.

"Ya was eying me very hard before boss. I thief your girl or sain?" He took a drag and passed the spliff to me on his exhale.

"Nah, I was just listening iya. Ya had nuff tings to say." The smoke caused my throat to burn; I exhaled and passed the spliff off to Ross.

"Safe. Safe." He caught me eyeing his watch but didn't say anything else for a minute. "It nice, right? You waan try it on?"

The opportunity caught me off guard and I was telling him yes before my mind had figured out if that's what I wanted to say. He undid the watch, slipped it off his hand and extended it to me. I took it, slid it on and fastened it.

"Dat's 'bout twenty-five right dey."

"Hundred?!" He chuckled at the surprise in my voice.

"Nah. Thousand, boss." I froze before looking down at how the watch, illuminated by the full moon, adorned my wrist. I took it off and returned it to him gingerly, the same time the spliff had gotten back to him.

"I used to look at things jus' how you looking at dis hay." He laughed again and traded me the watch for the spliff. I took another drag and passed it along as he kept talking. But unlike before, I was actually listening this time.

The spite had resurfaced once he'd told me the price of the watch. However, I now held some hope that maybe he would also tell me how he'd gotten the things he flaunted so freely and how he'd gotten to the place where owning them was no big deal.

He was getting ready to explain when he stopped smiling and made eye contact with me. "If ya willing ta run wid de big boys, dat's how ta get big boy tings."

Not making the connection immediately was honestly stupid of me. "Running with the big boys" is how everyone talked about selling drugs and "other stuff". Our island, while small, was a big international hub for all the debauchery in the world: drugs, humans and all kinds of extortion. They all flowed through the underbelly of the island, and were being used to fatten up our politicians. Before now, that way of living was behaviour I frowned upon. But the more I thought about it, the more I realized my perspective had changed. Because I would do anything if it meant I didn't have to be poor anymore.

"Boy right now fella, de devil could come and ask me to run wid de big boys and I would tell he yea'. Ya ain' know?"

It was my turn to get the spliff again and I took a giant pull. He doubled over laughing when I started to cough and I laughed too, as I tried passing it over to Ross who had fallen asleep propped up on a tree.

"Wuh's you name again?" I asked after I'd kicked Ross awake and handed the spliff over to him.

"Shawn."

Part Two

Chapter Six

THE OTHER GUY

It was three in the morning when Shawn dropped me off at the bottom of the road to my house. The same place Roddy had dropped me earlier in the day. I should have given him the route that would have spit me out closer to home but I was high, so when he offered to drop me home, I'd given him the directions I was used to taking.

"Yea' iya. I gine leh you know dis week." He beeped his horn twice, then sped off down the unlit road. I watched the red lights from the car disappear before I turned around to start the twenty-minute stroll towards my house.

Going home tonight was a completely different experience to this afternoon. First, it was no longer sweltering outside. Second, I was high out of my mind. And third, Shawn agreed to contact his boss for me, to ask if he had any openings. Combining those things made the walk more enjoyable and being in a good mood would make the time go more quickly.

I was halfway to the turn when the cool wind stopped blowing and a bone-deep, icy breeze wafted through the air. The hair on my arms stood up and it felt like someone was watching me. The eerie feeling lingered on the back of my neck and I absentmindedly ran my fingers across my nape to wipe it away. I glanced behind me in case I could make out anyone in the extreme dark, knowing the possibility was highly unlikely. When I turned around, he was standing there.

An unnatural stillness enveloped everything, except for the breeze that made it hard to move. For a moment I couldn't maneuver, as fear gripped my limbs and held me paralyzed. I took a deep breath before I started walking again.

The man wasn't budging and as I started nearing him, I slid my hand in my pocket so I could get a hold of the knife I kept there. My heart was beating out of my chest. I was maybe three feet away from where he was standing. He was taller now that I wasn't so far away, with broad shoulders; his stance was intimidating. I couldn't see his face but I pushed my chest forward and gripped the knife tighter as I got within range. There was no way to pass without walking right by him. But I'd made up my mind to stab him in the throat if he tried anything. Worst came to worst, I would rob him after. My fear had twisted into dread and I was prepared to attack when his unsuspecting laugh halted my plan.

"So much fear for someone who issued an invitation." He stepped towards me, closing the space, and I tried to step back further once I was able to see his face.

"Oh God."

He chuckled sinisterly and took another step closer so he could whisper into my ear. "Not Him. I'm the *other* guy. The one who heard you're accepting offers."

Chapter Seven

You Had An Offer For Me

"Nah bigman, watch ya cunt from round me." I stepped back to put some space between us and tried to pull the switchblade from my pocket. My hand didn't respond and it was a second before I noticed my entire body was frozen. He smiled, exposing elongated, golden fangs and shook his head as he stepped forward to eliminate the space I'd just created.

I wanted to scream. A terror like I've never felt before had snaked its way up my veins and demanded I cry out. He was terrifying and handsome, intricately and enticingly so. He tilted his head from side to side as we stood face to face while I stared into his pitch-black eyes; glowing red veins running through their infinite darkness. He straightened his stance and circled me like the predator I knew he was; stalking me with his movement, every action made me feel like feeble prey. Terror was making my heartbeat accelerate and deep within myself I *knew* I was going to die. A thought flitted through my mind; it ensured me that I would be glad to die by his hand. I felt like I was losing my mind. I needed to know what the fuck was going on.

"Don't worry, you'll snap out of it in a minute." His voice was amplified and distorted as it surrounded me. "Isn't it silly how you didn't ask for God's help but you thought He would respond. He doesn't, by the way. Not usually." He shrugged. "But me? I take direct invitations *personally*."

He was standing in front of me again. So close now that if I could move I'm sure I would have pissed myself. He extended a stiletto fingernail towards my face and sliced my cheek, drawing blood with the motion. It stung but I couldn't wince, and when he sucked the blood off his finger, I internally cringed.

"Stop acting like an adolescent." He rolled his eyes. "I'm here to make you a business proposal, not suck you dry. I'm nothing if not professional, and *you*, you had an offer for me. Remember?" He waved his hand dramatically towards himself at the same time he said the word "me".

"Now speak." The force holding me in place lifted; the instruction compelled me to engage in conversation.

"Boss, what de fuck you is?!"

"You know *who* I am. You called me by name earlier. Well, I guess you didn't *technically* use my name. But it's all the same." The echoing of his voice was becoming even more pronounced. "Don't waste my time boy!"

The authority in his voice made me flinch and I knew right then, against all possibility, that he *was* the devil. What did that one quote say? *"When you have eliminated the impossible, whatever remained, however improbable, must be the truth?"* Well, I felt it with my entire being that my assumption was the absolute truth. I was standing toe-to-toe with the king of hell, and he was here to call my bluff.

My voice was not like I'd ever heard it before and I had to clear my throat a few times before it sounded close to normal.

"I, I din mean—"

"Of course you did!" He stopped me from talking. "I wouldn't have come if you didn't want it with all your soul. I hear silly pleas all day long but I never come unless it's a *real* offer. I tasted it in your blood."

"Wuh I mean is—"

"You didn't *think* I would come because you didn't *believe* in my existence. But now I'm here and willing to give you a job where you can get what you want without needing to, as you put it, '*run with the big boys*'." A bench materialized in the center of the road and he sat down.

"Now listen up."

Chapter Eight

It'll Cost You Extra

"I need a new heartman in this area and that's going to be you." It was ironic that the job offer didn't sound like a request. "And because I know you're going to wonder, yes you can decline. I'm not unreasonable after all. Of course, refusing me will cost you your foot. However, I'll leave you alone after that. You won't be able to join Shawn anymore, *obviously*. And you'll die from an infection in five weeks." His attitude was flippant to say the least, and his smile was a menacing thing as he flashed his fangs again.

Suddenly, I felt a burning laceration move rapidly across the middle of my left calf; an incident that left me discombobulated as I went toppling over onto the cement. I screamed and grabbed hold of my thigh as blood gushed from my severed limb. I could feel it flowing out of me as it covered the ground in crimson liquid. My head exploded in agony and my stomach convulsed at the sight of my own blood. The pulsing pain from my missing foot was excruciating and black spots started to blur my vision. Through wide, watery eyes, I looked over at my cleaved off foot which had fallen over onto its side.

"Wuh de rasshole?! My fucking foot!" Every word was punctuated with unbearable anguish.

Then I was standing with both feet planted on the ground. The devil was cackling so loud it sounded like thunder. The shock of the moment was so overwhelming, it left me traumatized and speechless. I kept my eyes down, constantly putting more pressure on my left leg to confirm my foot was actually there.

"Now that you've refocused, here's the deal. I'll give you everything you want, you'll never have to wish for another thing in this life. And I'll throw in a little extra and make sure your family is covered too. Unlimited wealth and no health issues until the big guy calls your number. Untiil then you'll work *exclusively for me.*"

He didn't elaborate what "working for him" entailed, but I knew the story of the heartmen. They carved the hearts out of living people, usually children, and delivered them to the devil in return for whatever he promised them. I couldn't say no, well I could, but I'd lose my foot *and* I would still be poor before meeting my untimely end.

The temperature of the wind was still making my bones vibrate, and I kept reliving the devil's manifestation of my severed limb instead of concentrating on what he was saying.

"I can feel you wasting my time." He expelled a dramatic sigh, simulating detachment. But I could sense the frustration aggressively rolling off him. I was running out of time to decide. I was going to die someday anyway; I could at least provide for myself and my family before that.

"When I done, my family gine still be good? No matter what?" He let out an ominous bray at my question before he answered.

"I can make that happen but it will cost you extra." I nodded and he continued. "My quota for your request is three hearts a week. And because I'm being gracious by throwing in a four for one deal, I'll need the purest hearts possible. So, no one over nine."

My stomach cramped, horrified at the directive. But he didn't say anything else. He sauntered over to me and cut his palm open with the same nail he used to slice my face earlier. He took his thumb and rubbed it over the open wound, looking deep into my eyes. The smell of his blood twirled around my nostrils and I was repulsed that I unexpectedly became aroused. He waved his uninjured hand through the air dismissively.

"Focus!" He was as frustrated as I was disgusted by my confusing attraction towards him. "Do you swear to serve only me, to your dying day, in exchange for making all your financial wishes come true? Knowing that failure to meet your specific quota will result in a nullified contract?"

My acceptance of the agreement was quieter than I desired. I wanted to sound confident; I needed to convince myself that I was brave and not scared shitless. But if he thought I was a coward he didn't say anything. All I got from him was elation at my confirmation.

"Well done!" He anointed me with his bloody thumb before placing a kiss on my cheek that reminded me way too much of the story of Judas betraying Jesus.

"I'll be back to collect in a week. Make those hearts the sweetest little kiddies you can find." He winked and was gone before I could ask any questions.

I'd just made a deal with the devil to carve the hearts from the chests of little children. I sprinted over to the side of the road and puked into the cane field.

Chapter Nine

Hearts Beating In Tandem

The keys slipped between my shaking hands four times before I opened the front door, and I gripped them together tightly to stop their rattling once I eased inside. My heart hadn't stopped pounding and my stomach was doing somersaults. I'd vomited twice before I got home though it was only ten minutes from where I'd stopped.

When I closed the door behind me I could sense my family in their sleep. The way their hearts whispered to me was surreal; their heartbeats pulsing in my veins like each one was my own. The urge to procure one from its owner was so strong and compelling that I wasn't aware I'd pushed open the door to my mother's room until I was standing at the foot of her bed.

I walked around to the side where the woman slept and a dagger materialized into my hand, but it was the child next to her that called out to me. Her heartbeat was like thunder in my ears; it was faster and quicker than the older heart. Pure and untainted. The exhilaration propelled my feet from the left side of the bed to the right. Her heart was so close it made my mouth water. I ran the dagger up the length of the bed, feeling as it caught tiny imperfections in the cotton while creating micro tears. Then I was running my blade up her tiny arm, barely hovering over her skin, careful not to damage anywhere I didn't mean to. The child shifted, turning in my direction, her tiny eyes flickering open and landing on me.

"Mar-mar?" Her little fingers went up to rub one of her eyes as the dagger disappeared from my hand. The child knew me. It was confusing to watch the recognition dawn on her face.

"Mar-mar, wuh you doing?"

She sat up and I was struck by the disgusting revelation that this was my little sister. I had almost carved out her heart for the devil and I would have done it with no recollection. I stooped to soothe Kimberly's tiny frame back into a sleeping position.

"Just making sure ya was sleeping alright." I had to whisper so I didn't wake my mother. I comforted Kimberly until she went back to sleep and then rushed into the room I shared with my brother, almost slamming the door to put distance between my sister and me.

I'd broken out in a cold sweat and I felt nauseous again. But at least my sister was unharmed. For a split second, the adrenaline started luring me into a false comfortability, until I noticed Akeel. My brother's heartbeat sounded like racehorses in my ears, and I was repulsed at how badly I wanted to push my hand into his chest cavity and rip his beating heart out of it. I needed to put space between myself and the people I loved, so I started climbing through our bedroom window. My foot hit the grass of our miniature backyard and I slid against the cold, outdoor wall.

I could hear all of them out there; the hearts beating in tandem. Some faster and louder than others. They were calling to me, coaxing me into something I didn't think I could do.

I sat outside for a long time and as the sun started coming over the horizon, the pull of the hearts and the desire to kill abated. A sigh of relief made my chest swell and I held it for a minute before I released it. Then a heavy trunk popped into my lap. It was medium sized, made out of obsidian metal and carved with intricate detailing. When I opened it, a LED light illuminated three square-shaped, acrylic slots. There was an engraved message on the top that read: 'Time: 165 hours left'.

Chapter Ten

162 Hours Remaining

I'd never gone to sleep, and I didn't notify my family that I was hiding in a corner of the backyard. My mother was rushing my siblings along so they would be ready for the church picnic.

"Akeel, Jamar ain' home?"

"Nah, his shoes ain' at de door." I looked down at my feet for the first time, realizing I'd never taken my shoes off, as I eavesdropped on their exchange.

"He mussi ain' come home ya know so I hope he got his key. Nancy outside, lewwe go." I listened to the sound of the door closing and locking.

After a shower I felt a little better but I knew I was already running out of time. I opened the trunk again, looking at the three empty slots, the timer on the top was now showing I had 162 hours. I was exhausted and I needed a plan but I went to sleep instead.

The sound of voices entering the house stirred me awake. It was dusk, the light from the still-opened chest shone brighter since there wasn't much sunlight left. I'd lost an entire day when I should have been figuring this out, and now I was starting to lose focus as the setting sun was amplifying the heartbeats around me. I closed the trunk and walked into the living room where I met my family who'd just arrived.

"When you get home?" My mother was struggling with containers of leftovers from the picnic and I hurried to help her.

"Ever since but wunna was already gone." I placed the food on the table and slid my feet into my slippers; my hand was on the doorknob.

"Wait, ya gine out again?"

"Yeah, de men holding another lil' lime." My little sister ran into my leg and wrapped her arms around me. The sound of her heart had begun drowning out everything else, so I hugged her back quickly then pushed her away.

"Oirt, I out." I rushed outside before anyone else could hinder me from leaving.

It was around seven when a message popped up on my phone. I was aimlessly walking the streets, constantly tempted by the pulsing hearts inside each house I passed. I looked at the phone screen; Shawn was letting me know the meet up with his boss was a go for tonight at eleven. He told me he would pick me up where he dropped me off last night. I shoved the phone back in my pocket and kept roaming the road until a tantalizing heartbeat caught my attention.

I walked down the gap and turned left around a corner covered by overgrown bushes. I didn't know where I was going so I let the cadence of his beating heart guide me. He was six years old and tucked into bed. It didn't take me long to locate him, my pulse quickening to match his. The hankering to feel his warm heart in my hand kept growing the closer I got.

The house was moderate in size; I prowled pass the front along the side. The lights in the living room were dimmed as two hearts beat erratically. Besides the boy and his parents, there was no one else in the house, except a cat who was asleep in the laundry room. I pushed down on the side door's handle and it silently gave away under the weight of my action. My footsteps were soundless as I glided towards his room. The dagger emerged like it'd sensed my most intimate desire, and my fingers felt at home on its hilt. I pushed the door open and moved around the bed until I was standing on his right side. I extended my arm above my head, prepared to strike when his little voice broke through my compulsion.

"Daddy?" I backed away anxiously and darted out the door where I'd entered. I tripped down the steps and crashed into a garbage can. The noise I made pulled attention from inside and a security light outside flickered on, bathing the front of the house in bright white light. I couldn't leave the way I'd come so I turned around and ran in the opposite direction. There were no security lights at the back and I didn't hesitate to check why there weren't. I ran as fast as I could, letting the shadows of the foliage and building console me. I jumped over the fence and headed towards the main road. Once I'd gotten clear, I stopped running and hunched over so I could catch my breath. There was no way I would be able to do this; I couldn't hurt little children but I had a deadline to make, and if I didn't, I would *literally* have hell to pay.

Part Three

Chapter Eleven

A Major Jackpot

I spotted Shawn's car lights in the distance. I hadn't bothered to go back home to check the box — as long as I got the hearts I needed before time ran out, I didn't have to worry. There was only one problem: I'd established I couldn't kill who I was supposed to. Both times I'd failed, resisting the compulsion somehow.

I was angry at the predicament I was in. Who knew I should have taken my grandmother and her "power in the tongue" rhetoric more seriously. If I hadn't unknowingly called *him* with my loose lips, I wouldn't be standing here with no idea what to do. Children *should* be off limits, and they were for me, so that meant I would have to find another way.

The car was still coming down the road, so I started hatching a plan while I waited. The devil needed hearts, and he wanted children, but would he know if I got him something else? If I could obtain a few that belonged to some sheep or pigs, maybe I could resize them. Did their hearts look human? I was lost in my thoughts when Shawn screeched to a stop in front of me. He had a spliff and a drink and was screaming at me to hurry up and get in; his voice was barely audible over the blaring music. I walked around the back of the car, double tapping the phone screen to look at the time.

"Hurry up big man! De boss doan like when people late!" He was still yelling, though I was already inside and closing the car door.

Shawn's heart was doing a mile a minute and my supernatural impulse returned. I could carve him up easily if I wanted and that was perhaps something I *could* live with. He was a criminal after all; a criminal with a heart I could put in the first slot of my box. He took a swig from the flask he was holding as he sped through the streets in his attempt to make it to our location as quickly as possible. The dagger appeared in my hand and I tried to make it go away; I wasn't ready yet. But I'd decided at that moment. I would separate Shawn from his heart when the opportunity arose, then I would deal with the fallout, if there was any, later.

I was so focused on the thrumming of his heart that I didn't notice when Shawn pulled the car into a deserted parking lot. I looked up as we started slowing down and noted the two silhouettes waiting. As we got closer, the headlights morphed the two shadows into two men, presumably the boss and another employee. The idea consumed me at once and I knew I could turn this into a major jackpot if I played my cards right. Three men, three hearts. One night and I would be done days ahead of time.

We got out of the vehicle and walked towards the men; a larger one who was covered in tattoos, was using his body to partially shield the other—so he wasn't *just* an employee. The dagger hadn't gone away so I'd shoved my hand into my pocket. Shawn and I moved forward quietly, until the bodyguard put up his hand, signaling us to stop. I wouldn't be able to get the two of them if I was standing this far away.

"You're ten minutes late. I hate it when people are late." A thin, tall man stepped out from behind the burly bodyguard. He tried making his way to us when the bodyguard intervened.

"Distance, sir."

He silenced the bodyguard by waving his hand through the air. "Look at them. They came for work. Not to kill me." He smirked confidently where he stood, which was now directly in front of me.

The sound of his heart beating steady and strong told me everything I needed to know. He wasn't afraid; he was a man instilled with the audacity that no harm would ever come his way.

"Now who do we have—"

I didn't let him finish the sentence as I pulled the dagger from my pocket and rammed it into his carotid artery before viciously ripping it away.

Blood sprayed across my face and I licked my lips to taste its sweetness. Screams were coming from somewhere near me and the thunder of terrified hearts pounding was crashing into my skull.

A large outline was coming my way, it stalked forward with purpose and I knew it must be another man. But I could no longer make out his exact features; I could only see the outline of his heart. It was glowing and calling out to me through his shadowy frame. He lunged forward, but wasn't able to get to me fast enough. While he was reaching out towards me, I threw the dagger, embedding it deeply into his left eye. His heart lit up like Christmas. It's once stable rhythm now erratic, until he slumped backwards and stopped moving.

I leaped up and landed in a squat over his body, took the dagger from his eye and plunged between his fourth and fifth ribs, for added insurance. Then I craned my head towards the screaming.

Chapter Twelve

Stop Fucking Moving

The final heart was retreating. I could see its vessel fall and scramble up before it started running away again. The vessel's movements were turbulent and I found myself tilting my head back and forth to keep track. And while it was fun watching the vessel dart around, I wanted the heart too badly to wait any longer. I let the desire to catch the vessel fill my system and before I knew it, I was relocated directly in its path. It almost collided with me when I popped over and it let out a petrified scream before stumbling backwards.

I could see the terror-stricken heart and the sight of it was exhilarating. It sounded like fluttering hummingbird wings as it beckoned me to take it. The vessel was crawling away, unable to regain the standing position after falling. I stalked forward in happy pursuit, knowing it would not escape me.

"Stop fucking moving." My voice didn't sound like me. It was a raspy whisper; sinister and deep.

My prey froze instantly.

It didn't take too many steps before I was standing over it, then I crouched so we were face to face. The appetizing scent of fear was bombarding my olfactory system. I smiled and it felt like it stretched farther across my face than it should have.

A second dagger materialized into my other hand. I eased forward and knelt above the vessel, placing my knees on either side of it before I sat down. In its fear it was trembling; making noises that I could barely differentiate as being more than muffled nonsense. It probably thought I could understand what it was saying. But if it was communicating, I couldn't tell.

"Shhh." I pulled it into an embrace; daggers still clutched securely in my hands. I felt its heart hammering against mine.

The vessel thrashed violently in my grip but I didn't care. The only thing that mattered was the ecstasy of this moment; I didn't want it to end. But I had a job to complete. I could feel a timer somewhere waiting for me.

I shifted the vessel marginally, leaning it backward. I crossed my hands and placed them against its neck. I exhaled slowly and in one fluid, swift motion, I drew them across the shadow forcefully and the vessel's movement stopped. Its heart though motionless, still glowed brightly. I watched it for a bit until the glow started to dim. Then I got up because I still had work to do.

After dragging the vessels into a straight line, I made quick work of carving them up. Each of them was butter under my blades and I plucked their hearts from them for my collection. I walked back to the car so I could find something to carry them in, when the sight of my reflection in the window caught me off-guard.

My face was gaunt instead of rounded; my cheeks hollowed so deeply that my head looked like a skull instead of a face. I kept changing positions to make sure it was actually me. My eyes were glowing red like the devil's and when I reached out to touch the glass, long, thinned fingers reached out instead of my normal hands. I immediately recoiled, pulling my corrupted extremity back to me.

I searched the car closest to me and found an unused backpack in the trunk. I picked up the three hearts, shoved them inside the bag, then thought about walking home. I can't remember how I got there, or when, but it felt like I'd blinked and was now in bed. I didn't want to question it so instead of fighting the exhaustion, I let myself drift off to sleep.

Chapter Thirteen

True Relief

I stirred awake at around midday the next day, stretching out across my bed like a ginger cat. As soon as my eyes opened completely, the memories from last night assaulted me. I had killed Shawn, his boss *and* the bodyguard. And I'd done it as a monster. The experience was hazy in the beginning, the remnants of sleep clouding my memories. But the longer I stayed awake, the more I remembered and the clearer it became. At first the flashes felt like a dream, so distant I didn't think they were real. But by the time I had recalled it all, I knew with a certain bone-shattering clarity that everything I'd remembered, I'd actually done.

My sister was in the living room watching cartoons; I could hear her jovial giggles echoing through the house. Then my brother's voice pulled my focus away from her to him and his friends, who were outside whispering about something. Their hushed voices were coming from under the bedroom window.

"Dis gotta be he stash but I can' get it open." I dismissed them, reaching my hand under my bed so I could look inside the chest.

I didn't feel it at first and panic catapulted me to the floor where I got on all fours to properly search for it. It wasn't there, and a moment after discovering that, I figured out where it'd gone.

"Akeel, bring back my rasshole ting in here before I cut your ass boy!" I yelled through the window, eliciting laughter from his friends.

A couple minutes later my brother walked in, and dropped the black box on my bed. I knew he would have chucked it at me if he could have, but it was way too heavy.

"Yous doan gotta get on so." That was all he said before he stormed out.

I didn't know what to expect but I almost shit myself when I opened the box and the LEDs bathed the three hearts in light. I slapped the lid shut instantly, then took a deep breath before I opened it again. I looked at the timer carved into the lid, surprised I still had over five days left.

For the first time since my "employment", I felt true relief. The urge to collect hearts had decreased; I could barely hear them whispering now. I ran my hand down my face, surprised at the comfort this simple action gave to me. I smiled with the knowledge that there were still so many days left; proud I'd possibly found an alternative way to complete the job. No, I couldn't doubt myself if this was going to work. I'd completed the job *as requested*. I would have to coach myself into accepting this fact wholeheartedly. Then I would have to convince the devil.

I spent the remaining days trying to formulate the next step of my plan. If I cut the hearts down to size that might be enough. Or maybe he wouldn't look in the box. Then I considered the fact that the devil didn't *actually* care about the specific hearts all that much. He said it himself that he wasn't unreasonable.

My worrying officially stopped a day before my quota was due, when I checked the timer on the box and saw an engraved message that read "Prepayment incoming". My heart skipped a beat. I hadn't even delivered the hearts yet but the devil was about to pay up, lending validity to my assumption that he was more reasonable than not. My mother's scream shattered my train of thought.

"Jamaaaaar, ah win de lotto!"

I rushed out of my bedroom, knowing exactly how it happened and still simultaneously unsure that I heard her correctly. When I flew through the small archway between the hall and the kitchen, she was sitting at the table grasping the newspaper so tight, it was crumpling out of sight between her fingers.

"Mummy, you win?!" She nodded her silent response with happy tears streaming down her face and I had to pry the paper from her hand to compare it to the ticket on the table.

I compared the numbers five times just to make sure they were right, then I started laughing.

Chapter Fourteen

Sugar Cane Swaying

The next night I followed his instructions which sent me to the same spot I'd first met him. Then I waited for the devil to return; the weight of the chest made heavier as the possibility of disapproval still lingered in the back of my mind.

I'd decided yesterday that I would stick to my plan and only pivot if I needed to. But the longer I waited, the more nervous I got. There was a light breeze making the sugar cane sway, sending its earthy, sweet smell through the air. The scent was calming so I took a few deep breaths. When that didn't make me feel better, I started fixating on the chirps of the crickets as an added distraction.

I knew he'd shown up as soon as the abnormal glacial wind wafted around me and the crickets' stridulation disappeared. But I blinked and missed his arrival. Because now he was walking towards me; a smile plastered across his face.

"I won't ask if you got my payment." The look on his face told me there was no debating it even if I hadn't. "Now hand me my box." He extended his hand towards me and the chest I had been clutching protectively, flew out of my grasp.

He held it like it weighed nothing, balancing it in his palm. The lid automatically flew open.

"How old were the children?" He was inspecting the hearts, not looking at me.

"Am, I can' remember. I think eight, five and six." I'd spent hours rehearsing this conversation over and over.

"And they were *alive* when you took the hearts? Not corpses?"

"Nah. I mean yeah. All alive, well not alive afta I tek dem." He looked at me with an arched eyebrow so I kept talking. "Well, you know wuh I mean. Before I tek de hearts, dem was alive. *Afta* I had de hearts, dem was dead."

"And all children?"

"Yeah." The box slammed shut.

When he looked at me his eyes were flaming red, and a feeling of dread leaked from the pit of my stomach into my bloodstream.

"I am reasonable." The devil's words were punctuated as he circled me. "But the good book calls me the father of lies." He didn't break his stride as he spoke, his voice dangerously low. "And I," he paused to adjust his collar, "I am *thee* liar which means that it's stupid to fucking lie to *me*!"

Fear froze the blood in my veins before my body ignited in extreme pain. I tried to scream but I didn't have a mouth anymore. I glanced frantically from left to right as I tried to use my fingers to claw my mouth open. Horror washed over me at the sight of them; they were elongated and curved, the same way they had been when I'd taken the three hearts. The pain was excruciating but I kept slashing my face. I could feel blood coating my new fingers, but as soon as I would rip enough skin away for a scream to escape, the area would seal up again.

The devil was inconsolable as he laughed at my transformation.

"There's always one of you who thinks you can weasel your way out of our agreement with a ridiculously formulated plan." The joy on his face made his eyes twinkle.

Pain jolted my focus away from his taunting and back to my body which was still changing. My clothes had disintegrated and I looked down at my naked frame, now emaciated. My skin was pitch black; I looked like a shadow. All except my heart which streamed red light out my concaved chest.

"Your eyes look the same way as your new heart, if you were wondering." His smile was broad and ominous.

My memories were starting to slip away, and my family felt more and more like something I'd imagined. Then my limbs started to extend and suddenly I was standing forty feet in the air; my elongated arms stretching past my knees. *A thought lingered that there was somewhere, somewhere I was supposed to be. But I couldn't remember where that place was.*

"Hell. We're going to hell, my disobedient heartman." *And I knew that was true. Because I belonged to him and I would serve him forever.*

A portal opened right after shackles appeared around my hands and feet, and I was yanked forward through the gateway where I was greeted with blazing heat and agonizing screams. It might have been scary to someone else but it wasn't for me because I knew it was my home.

Chapter Fifteen

THE PERFECT CANDIDATE

I could feel their hearts everywhere as I watched them from the darkness. Master tasked me with bringing him the perfect recruit, a man that couldn't refuse his offer. They were so tiny from where I stood, but they moved around with human purpose, doing things for reasons I didn't understand anymore.

Memories sometimes drifted through my brain. Like clouds, I couldn't hold on to them and they were always gone before they really formed. I could vaguely remember that I might have had a family. But I no longer saw their faces; I didn't know their names.

I let my heart seek out the perfect candidate, rummaging through their desires one by one. I felt it double, then triple its rotation around the globe, before I found him. He was sitting at the side of a tombstone in an empty cemetery. I crouched down so I was as close as I could get. I needed to be able to listen to both his heart and his head.

"Ya left me long time now bro, but I still doan believe it." *He couldn't see me as I moved between the shadows of the setting sun.*

I sat my large body down on the opposite side to where he was. Every fiber of my being confirmed to me that he was an exceptional choice. The phone in his pocket started ringing and he pulled it out to answer it.

"Akeel here. No, no, yeah. I still coming." *He got up, brushed off his pants and headed to the exit.*

I didn't move immediately because I wanted to watch him leave. But when I got up, I glanced at the tombstone that had held his attention so reverently. It was simple, small and engraved with the words "Here lies Jamar Pilgrim" above a broken heart.

I got up and opened the portal so I could return to hell, with only one thought on my mind.

Master's going to be so proud.

Glossary

A Guide to the Bajan Dialect in Whole Lotta Heart

Afta – After

Car' him wid ya nuh. – Carry him with you please.

Dat – That

De – The

Dey – There

Dis – This

Doan – Don't

Does come – Comes

Fit – Outfit

Fuh – For

Ga – Go

Gaffs – Jokes

Gine – Going or I'm going to

Hay – Here

I liming wid de men – I'm hanging out with my friends.

Iya – friend (Jamaican slang) commonly used in Barbados.

Knocking – Fist bumping

Leh – Let

Lewwe – Let us

Lime – Kickback/Hang out

"Man fit hard hard ya!" – The outfit he's wearing is fire!

Mussi – Must be/Probably

Oirt – Okay

Rasshole – Barbadian curse word

Sain – Something

Slippers – Flip flops

Sus crioss shotta – Jesus Christ shotta (This is a common greeting between some male friends. Shotta is Jamaican slang for shooter. In this context it's similar to shot-caller.)

Ta – To

Tek – Take/Took

Waan – Want

Wid – With

Wuh – What

Wunna – Y'all or You (referring to a group)

Yous – You is (Standard English you/you are)

Acknowledgements

I want to thank my husband, my parents, and my friends, who continue to show up to support me.

To my street team, I have no idea what I'd do without you! Literally. Being a new author can be a lonely experience and you've all helped me feel so supported through the my journey so far. Thank you, thank you, thank you! And a special thank you to my admins—Trish and Madi—because without them, this version of my stories would have never been created.

And I've thanked her before but I'm always going to shout out Zoe, who made the cover art for two of the short stories included in this book.

Lastly, I want to thank you – the reader. If you're here that means you've finished the mini collection of my first published works and hopefully you enjoyed seeing different sides of me as an author. I hope something in this short collection moved you enough that your heart raced, or you giggled a bit. Maybe I even made you curse or gasp. And if you want to tell me, I want to hear so I hope you leave me a review. Yes, I'm one of those authors who reads theirs, for now at least.

The journey of being an author means that much more when you know your words are reaching readers. So again, thank you.

About the author

Chia lives almost exclusively among star-flecked skies and dragon-guarded realms, where gravity is optional and impossibilities are simply plot twists waiting to happen. A longtime word-smith with a razor-sharp wit, she's happiest when inventing new worlds, and steadfastly ignoring the mundane one we all share.

Off the page, Chia is as genuine as they come—quick to share a laugh, even quicker to share a cocktail, and always ready to champion another creative in the pursuit of their dreams.

Chia's writing is a nod to her roots, where characters come to life and imaginative, unpredictable stories unfold. Her books combine the thrilling awe of classic sci-fi with the magic and wonder of fantasy, leaving readers convinced that reality is, quite frankly, overrated.

Need a portal out of the ordinary? Chia's got you covered!

Also by

PRIMORDIAL

A Novella

When an abnormally high fever sends Sawyer Elias to the hospital, she's abducted by two women who reveal earth shattering revelations that will change the entire trajectory of her life. As Sawyer struggles to deal with what she's learned, she's mistaken for Samantha DuClane. The misidentification sets both women on a journey of shocking realizations. One of them has to come to grips with her shifting reality, while the other instinctively agrees to the life-changing opportunity.

And the rest of the world?

Well, everyone else is running out of time.

Made in the USA
Coppell, TX
04 February 2026